To Kathy then and Kathy now
and Kathy always

—B.S. DE R.

For Julian and Nellie

—R.K.

GOING FOR A WALK

Text copyright © 1961 by Beatrice Schenk de Regniers. Text copyright renewed 1989 by Beatrice Schenk de Regniers.
Illustrations copyright © 1993 by Robert Knox. First published by Henry Z. Walck under the title *The Little Book* First
Harper & Row edition, 1982. Printed in the U.S.A. All rights reserved. 1 2 3 4 5 6 7 8 9 10 ❖ Revised
and newly Illustrated Edition, 1993. Library of Congress Cataloging-in-Publication Data: De Regniers, Beatrice Schenk.
[Little book]   Going for a walk / by Beatrice Schenk de Regniers ; illustrated by Robert Knox. — Revised and newly
illustrated ed.   p.   cm.   Originally published: The Little book. Henry Z. Walck; © 1961.   Summary: A little girl
goes for a walk, greeting many animals on her way and meeting someone who becomes her new friend.   ISBN 0-06-
022954-3. — ISBN 0-06-022957-8 (lib. bdg.)   [1. Animals—Fiction. 2. Friendship—Fiction.] I. Knox, Robert,
date, ill. II. Title. PZ7.D4417Go 1993   91-43177 [E]—dc20 CIP AC.

Going for a Walk

by Beatrice Schenk de Regniers • *illustrations by Robert Knox*

■ HarperCollins*Publishers*

The little girl goes for a walk.

She sees a cow.

The little girl says *Hi!*

The cow says *Moo.*

The little girl walks on.

She sees a rooster.

The little girl says *Hi!*

The rooster says *Cock-a-doodle-doo.*

The little girl walks on.

She sees a pig.

The little girl says *Hi!*

The pig says *Oink*.

The little girl walks on.

She sees a cat.

The little girl says *Hi!*

The cat says *Me-ow.*

The little girl walks on.

She sees a dog.

The little girl says *Hi!*

The dog says *Bow-wow.*

The little girl walks on.

She sees a bird.

The little girl says *Hi!*

The bird says *Cheep.*

The little girl walks on.

She sees a sheep.

The little girl says *Hi!*

The sheep says *Maa-aa.*

The little girl walks on.

She sees a bumblebee.

The little girl says *Hi!*

The bumblebee says *Bzz.*

The little girl walks on.

She sees a little boy.

The little girl says *Hi!*

The little boy says . . .

So the little girl walks on
and the little boy walks with her
and they find a sandbox. . . .

And the little girl
and the little boy
play together
all the day long.

FINISH

START